T1-BLX-870

3 1994 01306 7068

SANTA ANA PUBLIC LIBRARY

D0577664

For my sister Christine. N.C.

For my grandchildren. J.G.

Cat and Fish go to see

Illustrated by
Neil Curtis

Written by
Joan Grant

Simply Read Books

J PICT BK GRANT, J.
Grant, Joan
Cat and fish go to see

$16.95
CENTRAL   319940 13067068

Cat and Fish were
friends who lived where
the land and the sea met.
They looked up and out
and wondered about
the world. They decided to find
out where the waves went.

The flying fishes led the way.
The waves *raced* towards a cloudy island.

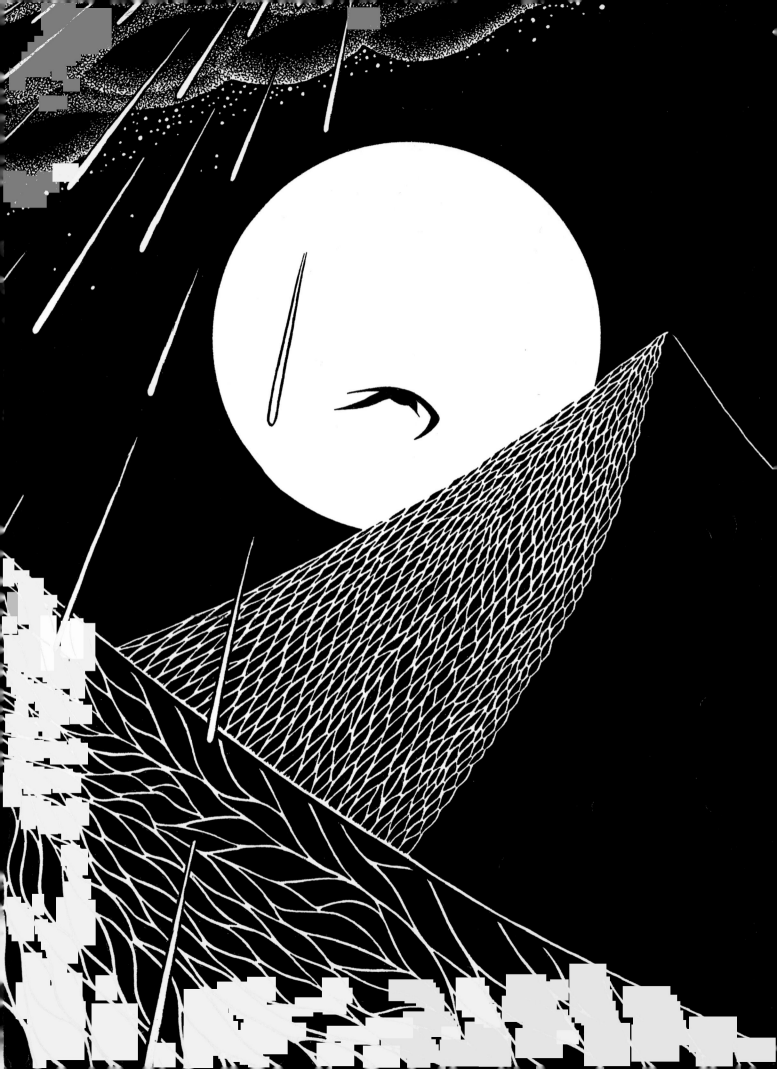

On the island

cat felt better; but where was fish?

The bold sea-eagle had
seen what happened.

He scooped fish up
and carried her to land.

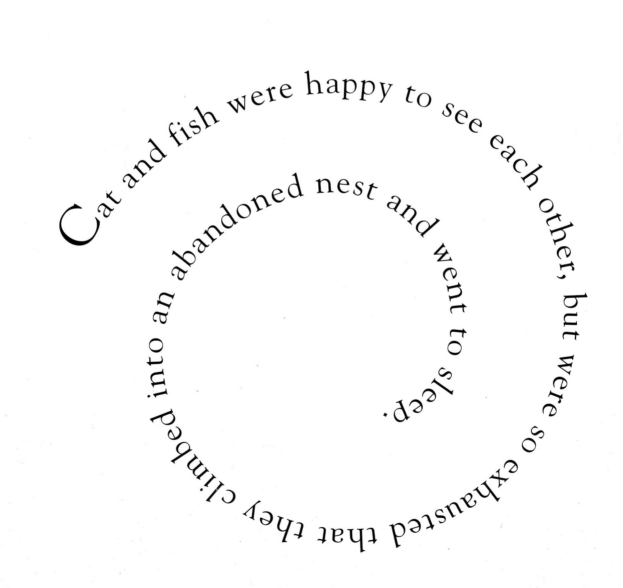

Cat and fish were happy to see each other, but were so exhausted that they climbed into an abandoned nest and went to sleep.

When they woke up they saw a lighthouse

and thought it would make a good lookout.

Cat watched the waves rolling far out to sea

and fish made wavelets in the bath.

They thought that if they
had wings like the sea-eagle
they could leave the island and
see where the waves went.

Fish asked the island's
twelve wise owls how
they could grow wings.

'Talk to the sea-eagle,'
the owls said, 'he has strong
wings to fly across the ocean.'

So
they
climbed
up to his
crag to
visit him.

Sea-eagle gave cat some
feathers to make wings, and
said fish could use his fins.

But cat got dizzy
and fish couldn't fly
high enough.

They tried to think of
other ways to change
and be more like each other.

'What if you could be a catfish,'
said fish, 'and I could be a fishcat?'

They imagined how they would look.

'But if

you were

a fishcat,

you wouldn't be fish,' said cat.

'And if

you were

a catfish,

you wouldn't be cat,' said fish.

They discovered they liked
themselves best the way they were:

A furry one who could run and

a scaly one who could swim.

They could be
better friends
than if they were
both the same,

and help each other follow the waves

to new adventures.

Published in 2006 by Simply Read Books
www.simplyreadbooks.com

Text copyright © Joan Grant 2005
Illustrations copyright © Neil Curtis 2005

First published by Thomas C. Lothian Pty Ltd

All rights reserved. No part of this publication may be reproduced,
stored in a retrieval system or transmitted in any form or by any means,
electronic, mechanic, photocopying, recording or otherwise, without the
written permission of the publisher.

Cataloguing in Publication Data

Grant, Joan, 1931-
    Cat and Fish go to see / Joan Grant ; illustrated by Neil Curtis.

ISBN-10: 1-894965-39-6
ISBN-13: 978-1-894965-39-2

    1. Cats--Juvenile fiction. 2. Fishes--Juvenile fiction.
I. Curtis, Neil, 1950- II. Title.

PZ10.3.G77Cat 2006   j823'.92   C2006-900131-6

Designed by Georgie Wilson

Illustration media: pen and ink
Color reproduction by Publlishing Prepress, Port Melbourne
Printed in Singapore by Imago Productions

10 9 8 7 6 5 4 3 2 1